FIRE IN PARADISE

ELIZABETH BAYOU-GRACE

STEVEN LEWIS

CODHILL PRESS

CODHILL
PRESS

Codhill books are published by
David Appelbaum for Codhill Press

codhill.com

FIRE IN PARADISE

Published in the United States of America

ISBN 978-1-949933-15-4
Cover and Book Design by Jana Potashnik
BAIRDesign · bairdesign.com

FIRE IN PARADISE

ELIZABETH BAYOU-GRACE

STEVEN LEWIS

CODHILL PRESS

NEW YORK · NEW PALTZ

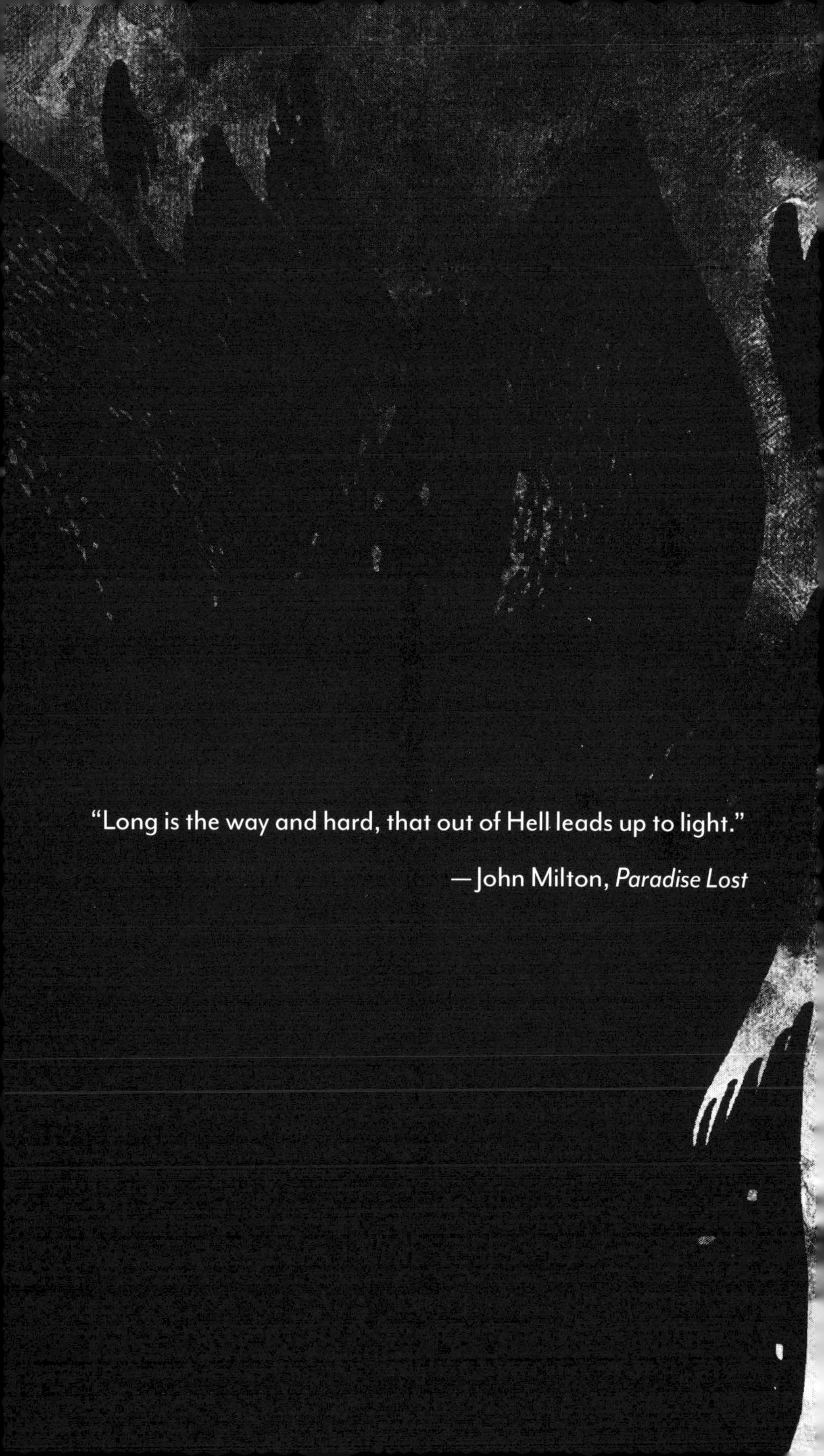

"Long is the way and hard, that out of Hell leads up to light."

—John Milton, *Paradise Lost*

CONTENTS

FOR RYAN AND PATTI

INTRODUCTION: ELIZABETH BAYOU-GRACE

And I see: Pound was an axe,

/ Chen was an axe, I was an axe,

/ And my son a handle...

– Gary Snyder

Among other identities, I am the daughter of a poet. When I was small, poetry was mostly a game. Daddy asks me to do the one about the plums and I oblige, "This is just to say...", or the wheelbarrow and if I forgot that the chickens are white, I start over. If I do it well and right, the joy on his face beams. Even if I do it wrong, we are sharing a moment between just us. I am my father's baby girl. Life is good. We do mostly William Carlos Williams. But sometimes, we do the ice cream poem and if I close my eyes and really focus I can hear the sounds: con, cue, piss, ant, curds. To me, it's all complete nonsense. I might as well be memorizing jabberwocky. Almost twenty years later, when I am reading the entire works of Wallace Stevens for my MFA, I find for the first time in print, "The Emperor of Ice Cream" and if I close my eyes and really focus, I hear all the sounds.

Over the years poetry has been many things to me: a party trick, a life raft, a secret language, an illuding muse. I learned about Sharon Olds from the poster in his office in the attic. Emily Dickinson from a book left with no explanation on my pillow in high school. Lunch Poems when I was woozy from morphine, post hip surgery. James Wright driving across the Wallkill, heading home.

So, to say that my father's voice is in my head when I write is an understatement. Chief sits in the room, in his daily uniform of jeans and a band tee, one leg crossed over the other, always. In his Buddha voice, he's telling me to trust the leap. Telling me that I'm getting in the way of what the poem wants. Telling me what poems to read again, what essays might have answers. There are days when I've pushed him from the room. Covered my ears and hopped into the void alone, wanting desperately to be a radical artist, a visionary, someone other than Steve Lewis's poet daughter. I have wanted to write without a giant on my shoulders. Other times, he's been my first reader. The poet I trust the most when he suggests that I cut the second half of a poem completely.

This has demanded a sort of neutral agreement about honesty between us. I read love and sex poems written to and about my mother. He reads a rotating cast of bad ideas and dangerous characters. We meet each other as father and daughter, teacher and student, fellow writers in this dangerous wild world. Sometimes, we're strange mirrors. I called him recently to discuss the idea of writing past events in present tense, because "time isn't real anyway". He laughed and said he'd been thinking the same thing. A few weeks later, I read his newest novel, a work that deals with the construct of time and how flexible it really is. Forty years difference, eighty miles away, and still we are reflecting back at each other.

My father and I started talking about making a split collection of poetry together shortly before the pandemic began. And then he was hospitalized with Covid-19, and we all watched the world change. Together. Separately. I began to understand how important it was to share our voices in the same collection, to be read together. To not only write with him in the room, but to explicitly invite him in. To make something beautiful out of our conversation. To suffer together. To learn together. To dream of a better world.

FIRE IN PARADISE

The first time I saw Texas on fire, dazed
and complicit in the driver's seat, her

clouds rising out over the back of hill
country rising, I thought for a moment,

with such relief: rain.
A break from the sun

and never setting. Maybe by tonight,
I thought with such relief, we'll sleep. But fire

was eating whatever wind it may. I
used to think living forever young was

the endgame. Under sun, the years swift pass
unnoticed. Fake plastic trees live longest.

No one will tell you when you're growing sick,
Elizabeth. They'll say thin. Have you seen

how the summer brays and flaunts? Vogues and screams.

DRIVING PAST THE CORNER OF COMFORT & PARADISE

the day as toasted as skin.
my hand firm on your
knee. we have come from the lake. between us we own
few things, just a stick shift and enough gas to make
it further on. we do not
own this lake; we do
not even belong to each other. lately, there
comes the distinct feeling, not of being emptied,
but that we always have been. how sweet it is
to owe you nothing. near to us, a young buck lifts
his head, as bared as we.

TWO-STEPPING

Breathless? Yes.
Whipped like moonlight milk froth, poured over nesting doll skeletons.
Babe,
I love your cowboy boots, pearl snaps, tall-glass-of-water kinda body.
You fill me
up slow speech, cursive lettering-
like wait. Wait. Wait for it.

DEAFSKY

The wideness of the sky in Texas
is deafening. The clouds tremble at / against the hours.
Tender poor
to find some wet.
The total sun could drive a girl mad.
Here. Here, here.
Outside the sky, there is only more space. Whole rooms of nothing.

BACKWARDSING

So, the highway blossomed into
Return— let's not call it failing.
See instead:
Magnificent backwardsing.
I love
your bad habits,
your sugar teeth. My soda pop
queen. You looked love in the face &
knew him. Good eye. You drank the good
stuff. Lasso the horizon in
to your tiny lap & drink at
it. Choose: loud mouth river city.
Say, let's make out more or why not?

DESTROYING THE THING WE LOVED

First, the garden went. August in Texas,
only the peppers could withstand the heat.
Without you, knee bent, laying down fish guts
as if it were the most delicate act

of praying, the ground split open so no
roots could take hold. Then the rest of the yard
weeded and burned. When the city turned off
the lights and water, or when the toilet

quit flushing, or the royal blue wagon
sputtered, bucked and stilled finally, all these,
I nearly begged you home. Instead, I spun
quicker, taking down the dishes, ripping

apart the plasters. In spring, we slipped soft,
unperceivable. By fall, disaster.

"WHEN THE PARTY'S OVER"

Either side of the road is flagged with farmed fields,
and beyond, in either direction, cradled inside soft
old hills. When I was young, I swore I'd hike
my way out of Appalachia. Either by foot, or by will.
And away I'd stay. Once I nearly caught a bus full of
psychedelic marching band players and a man on stilts
headed for Ohio. I made it all the way to Texas, once.
I never made it to California, in any real capacity, never
full blown manifest destinied, just a manic heartbroken
run once. The Yuba valley was riddled with gold flakes
and the men offered me marriage and LSD-and handfuls
of poems and gibberish. Still, distance is a funny thing,
I could be stretched so far. I could have pieces of my heart
in the Hudson Valley, I could be leaked and left
in a farming college in the Blue Ridge, I could find
my great grandmother's hometown in Mississippi and find
me there too, and Texas too, I could find a home stretched
thin like that. And I could love someone on the West Coast,
but I couldn't love them enough. There was a tearing point.
When a garment tears along the seams, it's an easy fix.
Even if it has frayed. When the tear is in the middle of the cloth,
most mending is, at the very least, visible. The way
the fabric reaches and stretches and moves on the body
weakens. I was weakened. There's a myth that says
if you step foot in the muddy Wallkill, you'll die there too.
I gambled a little further north. At least, I bargain with
my younger self, it's a different stretch. Smaller
but just as fresh. I bargain with my younger self, you weren't
so bright then anyway. You would have, for instance, ignored Billie Eilish
for her sheer popularity, and you would have been wrong.
I bargain with myself, the party lasts too long anyway. I'm driving
slowly through the Pioneer Valley. I almost know these roads
by now. I almost know all the words to the song. I'm singing
confidently enough. Driving confidently enough. The mountains
are stunning, spring looming. I could die here. That'd be okay.

REMEMBERING THE DAY BEFORE MY MARRIAGE

Most people are disappointing.
Around me, the ones I have loved fail
to rise and become. Great brains pickled
in jars, to be placed on a shelf.

As if to be used later.
Saved for good company. Silver locked up
in glass cabinets. My mother,

she used to only use the good silver
for the holidays, but she liked
the way it felt on her teeth
better, and one morning
she put it all in the regular drawers.

The silver gets tarnished, a little ugly,
but it still feels better on the teeth.
The good stuff becomes daily wear.

I think for a while there,
I was hoping all the good stuff was to come.

R. was dancing in kitchen / bedroom
in Little Pink House by the river,
as he made us one last late-night snack
before we slept unwed
for the last time.

We took it all off the shelves.
The good stuff.
The daily wear.

THE FIRST WINTER

Some mornings I have to remind myself that it will all grow back,
no matter how unlikely that seems. The grass is browning
under a layer of alternating melting and icing snow.

My mother calls me to ask if I'm surviving the winter. She wants
to hear both answers. Yes, and no, I've always been your southern
child, can we turn up the heat? Instead, R. adds another log.

And of course, yes. As a mother does. Hopes for unimagined
successes. Hopes for family. Even when it isn't snowing,
the air sometimes ices through and the wind turns solid,

white. The slick surfaces. It's always a hard winter, the first one.
The doctors said the PAO would give me another ten
to fifteen years on my feet. At 19 and 21, those odds

were favorable. I wasn't entirely sure that I would therefore
need another. She wants to know if the winter
is sitting inside my hips. Yes, and no. I can feel

the temperature sink, the frost in the blood. As if by
clockwork, the years have passed and I'm struggling
to lift. To rise. To walk those miles. Sometimes,

the valley swallows up all the warmth and the surrounding
Seven Sisters get capped in clarity. A little warmer
there at the glorious freezing top. Before I know

it, everything will be green. Despite me, or with no
regard to how I fare, winter will cease.

HIDDEN LAKE, SHAWANGUNK MOUNTAINS, NY

Hidden Lake is working herself
to freeze. Fractals blooming on her
surface. Here, now—this is real wealth.
Hidden lake is working herself
toward death. I gaze down her shelf.
Fullness of suspended treasure—
Hidden Lake. Working herself
to freeze fractals. Blooming on her.

SOME DAYS I WANT TO DIE

Some days I want to die, but I don't run
there. I'm not saying I should be praised but,

at least, forgiven. Like soft. Like I've left
the front door unlocked, I've left the porch light

on. Whenever you come home, come in. I've
been wearing you, love, like a fever dream. On

my haunches, peeling back the floorboards, I know,
peeling back the eyelash, eyelid. Wearing

you like a sick, ice sweat polyester sheet
stuck to sick, ice sweat outspoken spinal

obtrusions. Wearing you like something I
know I will have to peel off, peel back, lemon

in the tiny cuts. If you want to come
home, I won't die. I'll leave the door open.

FIRST SPRING IN MASSACHUSETTS

Every day a new color
appears in the yard.

First, malbec pearls on the shortest
spiney tree in front, overeager.

The old man neighbor with the perfectly
and often sculpted topiary

waves from a safe distance, says
the flowers should be here soon.

Next, milk lace like votive palms
rise near the door.

By Monday, I count six separate
shades of yellow. The farms

in the neighborhood are tilling
and seeding their bounties,

are mixing their palettes,
brown into green into hay into bounties.

Even when the world is, otherwise, stilled,
I find nothing is still. There is an unfolding.

This morning, the wine pearls flatten
to a bloodier red, while a single fire bud

persists, eager to bloom, by the bedroom window.

ON THE DAY WE LOSE COUNT OF WHAT DAY IT IS / CLOUD VILLANELLE

I trapped a cloud in a mason jar.
Right there on the coffee table,
let the smoke fill the entire reservoir.

Little reckless god moves, creating war
between what is temporary and what is stable.
I trapped a cloud in a mason jar,

the afternoon felt long, but evening was still far.
For moments it bloomed in its glass cradle.
I let the smoke fill the entire reservoir,

stilled the room, the moment even longer.
I am alone and strange in this valley of maples,
I trapped a cloud in a mason jar,

a little less vibrant in the fall bizarre,
my cloud and I suspended and disabled.
Let the smoke fill the entire reservoir,

let the still fill the room, spill over the floor,
a god and her cloud lit and unstable.
I trapped a cloud in a mason jar,
let the smoke fill the entire reservoir.

PRACTICING SAYING GOODBYE

This morning the cat woke me & there I
was surrounded by all my own things so
this morning I practiced loneliness. I
turned on the lamp, poured the coffee, back porch
sang myself back into body. The cat
thought to join me; didn't. The neighbors, back
fence to the trailer park, in response,
turned on radio hits from the last decade.
If I am true to my guts, then goodbyes
must be mostly permanent. In the start,
missing someone is easy. It's just there.
An emptiness to coddle instead. To
fall for. The work begins before that first
moment of break. Practice small. Imagine
one day of nothing between the lovers.

JOHN PRINE AND I SAT DOWN IN MY CLOSET WITH ALL MY OVERALLS

We huddled there, in the little gap between the shelves
and the shut door, curtained together
in the denim and canvas.
I was trying to catch my breath,
the news cycle was spinning too fast
again, and the phone wouldn't quit buzzing,
everybody was dying.

We talked about heaven. I said, heaven
isn't a word we use in this house,
and god isn't someone I would open arm
welcome these days. But when I get to heaven,
he said.

We sat for a while, and when I grew restless,
we opened the top shelf boxes,
the letters, photos. I remember everything,
things I can't forget. A lyric
for every occasion. My daddy wrote me a letter,
my sophomore year of college. I can tell I've
found the right one, simply by the weight of it.

We sipped our vodka and ginger ale,
while the world spun faster, gaining heft and speed,
and we waited to see the man in the moon,
hanging in the corner of the little dark closet.

Some men die, but they leave behind evidence of their living.
There is a lyric for every occasion.
A poem for every moment.
A letter I keep clutching.

44 WAYS OF SAYING I MISS YOU

I think I misspoke on that last phone call—
Don't get me wrong, I miss you more than I can say—

I love you like a lover, sister—
I'm worried—
I'm worried I hurt you—
I'm worried I stumbled over myself—
I'm worried about the state of the world—
I'd go to the ends of the earth to see you, but I can't go to Texas—

You raised me, Mama—
I'm angry with you too—
It's been a while—
I didn't know if I could say this out loud—
I'm a coward—

I feel like I'm losing all the people I loved—
I feel like I'm losing you—
More than anything, it boils down to you being brave—
More than anything, it boils down to me being fearful—

I'm sorry if I hurt you—
I'm sorry that I'm missing your child grow—
I'm sorry I left you—
I'm sorry I can't drink whiskey like I used to—

About what I said, it's not really about Covid—
It is sort of about Covid—
I miss you but I'd rather miss you than see my ex—
Our friendship is a gem I value—

I feel about Texas like you feel about Carolina—
The whole city feels soaked in the sweat of me running—
Austin smells like the little bits of me I've lost—
It feels like coming home a failure—
Remember when we used to skip class and eat Sonic?—
Remember when lived in the same tiny room?—

Just so you know, the quilt hangs in the guest room—
Just so you know, there are at least five airports in driving distance—
The world is crazy and I'm struggling to navigate—

I love you but—
I'm sorry, but—

Sometimes, when I run errands, I imagine you in the front seat, I say this is the cemetery, this is the dispensary, this is my favorite coffee shop, this is my favorite pond—
You're always with me—
I'm always with you—
I'm sorry and I'm not—
Is this my fault?—

I want to be honest with you—
We could meet someplace neutral like Canada—
Let me try and explain myself—

I WANT TO WRITE SOMETHING OTHER THAN ELEGIES

A love poem, for instance, in perfect
iambs and rhymes so near but not and all
the things unsaid in that tiny, empty,
misplaced space. I want to paint the bouquet
of peonies my husband woke early
in the morning to fetch for me, I want
to move the vase all around our home, want
the exact light. I want to be precise
and deliberate, and joyful. But they
keep creeping into the frame. The sick.
If I could, all my poems would be about
being 23 in a big city
in a house with my best friends. Rent is cheap,
we never need to sleep. But still, the sick leak in.

@ FRANK O'HARA RE: CITRUS

For instance—
An orange is an orange.
Born by trees
in warm wet tropics. Mostly
I buy one
from the supermarket, waxed
and tagged. Juiced.
Encased in Plastic. Sometimes
the orange
is a gift. Offered. A box
of oranges
from Florida to New York.
But if I
think about the juice sticking
to my chin,
then, the orange becomes a
memory.
The orange in my head is
constructed
of composite images
of oranges.
It's shape, approximate. Taste,
color, too.
It's unblemished. No tilted
nipple, bruise.
I can't eat the orange in
my head. The
orange in my head is not
the orange
in the hanging basket in
my kitchen.
I bought it when this mystic
told me I
might die before I get old
enough to send
boxes of oranges to those
born of whom
I bore. She tells me I should
spend time with
fruit. But not apple. Apple's
too much god,
so we settle on oranges.
But I get
to thinking. I get to thinking
about you,
Frank. Then the orange, even
in my hand,
becomes too heavy to hold.

SITTING ON A YARD RUG

It's a rare fish that knows it swims in water. – Proverb

Moved it outside. The yard grass high & ribboned. Listened to closely,
the world has an under voice. Sweet as—lovesick as—tiny jasmine
blooms from last season. Utterly
pleased to know itself. I've made all these grand gestures,
fruitless. Moved worlds in & between my fists. Still the sun
pulses upward, lightly. Despite
me. & then settles. So that globes
of brightness get caught in thicker
air. Willfully suspended. I
might demand a mountain out of
the hill country & be loosed by
grief. Or that the ocean may be stilled, & find myself nauseous against
it.

LOSS VS. IDEA OF LOSS

1)
It's almost like summer lasts too long.
The heat persists, and the oceans grow overconfident
like teen boys and the desert grows drunk on itself.

Sometimes loss is too much to bear
when it is many. I can't understand what it means
when an entire island is wrecked.

2)
A lot of lonely men call themselves islands.
A lot of lonely men are just
bodies. I got inexplicably angry

minutes before I found out that heroin
always wins. Takes 'em. Sometimes
leaves them just bodies. Sometimes

just statistics. Ideas. I want to grab
them by their wrists, the bruising, pulling
of a child out of a busy street . . .

3)
Guns don't kill people, people kill people.

Mr. President, that's the problem.

FEBRUARY 23, 2021

Admittedly, numbers are a language I am not conversationally
comfortable with, but this morning when I read
Heather Cox Richardson's Daily Apocalypse Update
while still sleep-warm and nested into my covers,
I could not fathom what 500,000 meant.

I think to myself, it's my duty to weigh these numbers.
As a human. As a poet. As a daughter. As an American. As someone
who has lost someone. Duty to bear witness, bear losses weight, bear
the guilt of surviving, of being complicit, of being inconsequential.

In classrooms, we've argued about whether or not poetry should handle
politics. We want our art pure, timeless. We want our poems
without cellphones, without names, without pop music.
We want our poems to be clean little
universes. Snow globes with an anonymous figurine.
We want our poems to bleed from battle,
but not wheeze with illness. We want our poems to bleed,
but not our blood.

Today's total Covid-19 death toll is 500,000.
I have four tall windows in my bedroom that open
to a wooded backyard, a single string of globe lights
across the pond, the snow still settling from the night's
quiet storm. The world is a snow globe. A poem.

I think to myself, I'll do something conquerable, like write
a poem with a word for every Covid death. I think I'll do something
easy, like say all of their names. I think I'll finally write a poem for
Arun. I think I'll give every person mourning someone a dollar. I'll apologize
for not keeping in better touch. I'll do better today.

But. 500,000-word pieces are life's works.
500,000-word novels kill men. I will stumble over names I am not familiar
with, and I will become dry mouthed,

and I will need breaks to weep,
and breaks to drink, and breaks to crawl into small, dark spaces.
My poem for Arun will not soothe his family. I think
I will die writing the same poem
over and over again, trying to fix it. To make it do it something
good, worthy. Make it something that can bear that much weight.

APRIL'S STORM FOR DUANE MARK

I try not to make weather into some karmic symbol.
I try to remember all the stormy days that were not fraught
with death or loss or pain. Sometimes the sky just breaks
open, wetting the windows, the roads, the hardy daffodils
that show up unexpectedly, and no one dies or has left,
and there have been temperate, even warm days, even
magnificent sun and bloomed white magnolia trees,
and we were losing, had lost, were mourning. But it is raining.
And the rain, the cold, is persistent. It even spring snowed.
I remember the rain on my grandfather's funeral (presumably
the realest first loss). I remember the rain that followed
Frankie. The wet day I made my way down the street to not mourn
Victor alone. We buy a meat smoker as the rain kicks up,
R. builds it in the living room. It's a few days until we expect
we might see sun, might be able to do the brisket justice.
(But it is raining).

INVASIVE PLANTS, ETC.

It's creeping in, overtaking again. In the fall,
we had our blind faith as we unrooted the vines

from around the front porch. I'm wondering when
we stop being newlyweds. Certainly, the first year,

every day is fresh and new. Our first hotel stay. Our first
home. The first time we kiss in the shower, married.

The first time we don't kiss in the shower, married.
The first fight. The first real fight. At first, all that blooms

in our first home's yard is sacred. Is breathtaking.
The burning bush, the skinny tall Norway Maples, the swallow

wort and her gothic tiny blossoms. The milkweed crowned
with butterflies. The leaning cherry tree. Then we began

to dig. Identify. Invasives abound. The second year felt
mostly new too. Today, we are fighting. I am unsure

if I am picking a fight because I feel wronged or because
the voice that roots inside my chest is flowering again.

At first, I think we have done a good job weeding.
An occasional swallow wart vines up near the fence lines

that we pluck with ease. We get busy. Lazy. Firsts becomes
seconds become routines. The pods swell and spread.

We strangle the remnants in garbage bags and bake
them in the sun. Our second anniversary is this week.

I'm wondering if I'm lying to people when I say I recently
got married. I'm wondering if 2020 doesn't count. Or

counts for a decade. Every time the voice quiets,
I think I have won. I think I'll never have a downturn

again. I'll get normal levels of sad. Not dangerous.
A single pencil-thin Norway that I can snap under my

fingers. Not a forest. I'm wondering if there is any way
to stop the spread entirely. Can I burn down the yard?

Can we time travel and leave all the spores in their appropriate
lands? Can we pause here for a while before we get

older? Can I smother the seeds if I believe enough?

HISTORY

I knew you before this. We were once un-
born together in a great mother, like
cream pearls were once wicked sand in the throat.
Then, we were the first people, descendants
of trees. I braided your hair while you pressed
moss, green velvet, against my chest. I named
you & you named me & we found language
so we could sing into the loneliness
of love. Last time I met you, we were small
things; we were children shining buttercups
yellow on our wrists. One morning I woke
to you cross-legged, sitting in my palm.
It was the summer solstice. Drunk with sleep,
I nearly mistook you for a wood nymph.

RESIDENTS OF THE MULTITUDES

I contain multitudes and the multitudes
contain me. I know this. I know I'm a single
grain of sand in a universe that I don't understand
the limits of. I know there are infinite stars and
infinite galaxies that are born and burn out
and collapse inside of my blood.

And when I'm calm (for instance, when I'm young,
in an empty cow pasture cradled in the blue ridges
that roll out like soft arms and breasts, that reminds
me of good mothers, when my heart is learning love
and fearing dying), then this is a comfort.

*

If I get to choose the guest list,
then my table
is long and heavy wood
and it seats my heroes:
the grandmother I never
met, Frida Kahlo, Greta Thunberg,
Mary Oliver, the little girl I once
knew with the hole in her heart (and when
we lost touch, how I never knew if she had
died or we had simply grown away, as grown ups
do), Jane Goodall.
Our table is heavy wood,
and benched,
and our meal is poetry,
animal fat, fresh spring ramps,
beets that stain our lips and tongues, and we eat
without guilt, fear. When, after the meal
is done, and we are full and honeyed

and softened to each other, we share
stories of other women we have admired,
and when I tell them I see how we
fit inside each other, simultaneously,
we nod.

*

It’s not that simple. You don’t get to pick and choose
the way the night/life unfolds.
If it
unfolds.

*

If I have the muse come to visit me, and inside of me,
then I have the bratty bored dumb child, come and here too.

If I have my love be a good man with ethics and heart,
and I have this man inside of me and we are the same,
then I have his brother too.

If the radical freedom givers, then the Nazis too.

*

Most of the time when I dream, I’m me.
But last night, at the 2 and the 3 and the 4,
I woke very aware I had been living
in the world, no matter how briefly, as a man.
I name myself Elijah so I can keep that moment
and remember myself.

*

The first time I remember reading Gary Snyder,
my father had given me a copy of Axe Handles.
I was in high school.

>

The first time I heard the word interpenetration
was in Sam Scoville's class
called Dialogue and Dialects at Warren Wilson College
in a tiny room with no windows and there was Sam
and his six weird baby philosophers alternating between
almost scratching through the curtain,
and absurdity and butt farming, and once
confronting that yeah, Dan and I were acting weird
because we'd gotten a little handsy
in a tent that weekend.

The first time I understood the word interpenetration,
I was reading Gary Snyder for a class in Texas
in a little cabin in the hills south of town with a skinny
wannabe Buddha, and suddenly all the words
I had been trying to say instead of god were
on the pages in my hands and they had once been trees
and seeds before that.

*

I've had multiple dreams involving Donald Trump.
In one, he was an old Scandanavian woman
who was angry I was picking flowers in her field.
Her field. In my dream.
The audacity.

I have never dreamt about any other presidents.
Carl Jung says every person in your dreams is you.
Everyone inside of me is me too.
Everyone inside of me is living outside of me, holding me,
holding all the different mes, the Elijahs, the monster presidents,
the dream dinner party, the good poets, the molesters
and my abuser. The whole gang.

I wake up from my most recent Donald Trump dream
extra upset that if I believe any of my own beliefs,

then we're all mirrors reflecting back at each other.
and when I read the day's news and scandal
and murders and trials and men shot by police officers
and children gassed and rapists still taking office,
I'm reading me over and over again.

*

It's too much to bear.—

This is something I like to say when I don't want to think about it anymore.

*

I have this recurring daydream where I name my abuser, and then I walk away. The scene varies. Sometimes he comes to whatever town I call home, and it's my turf, and I turn to someone who loves me or at least loves me more than a violent stranger, and I name his crimes. And I tell him to leave, and never come back. I claim my home and my space and my allies and somehow after this I am less hurt, less claimed. Sometimes, it's the dive in my hometown and I am showing someone I love the spaces that shaped me. I am explaining Snug's Surprise when one of the sweet but awkward boys I knew in high school approaches me. He'll say something like, didn't you used to date a rapist? and I say, oh, I did, is that monster here? I say, he raped me. I let the sweet but awkward boy know what company he keeps. I turn to my companion and I say, let's leave. And we do. And after, I applaud myself for being so mature, so nonviolent, so brave, so rectified, so healed.

*

I swear I have written
a poem before
about my daydreams

I wonder if this is a lie
I have told myself

>

I wonder if my daydream
has progressed
into the victory
of telling my naming
story

I swear I was in the sun
room and yesterday
they had stormed the capitol
and I couldn't

hear another violence
without it being
my violence

*

Patriot, according to Merriam-Webster,
means one who loves their country.

It is a word derived from the Greek
Patrios; of one's father.

Brethren. Men you war with. Countrymen.
Sometimes, it implies valor.
Sometimes strength. Usually, victory.
In 1776, the Patriots won the war.

In 2017, 2018, 2019, the Patriots won
the Superbowl. All hail the athletes.

In 2021, the Patriots stormed the capitol
and somebody shit in the hall.

*

In the first spring in our first home,
R. buys us a flag pole. I have never hung

a flag in my yard. We hang the progress
pride flag, and R. irons out the wrinkles.

Three doors down, the neighbor sports
two flags: Trump 2020, the confederate flag.

Across the street and down a ways
is a dove and the planet.

The Betsy Ross.

The United States of America.

Biden 2020.

Black Lives Matter.

Peace.

*

I moved to a town with more queer folks than proud boys.
I have a little Utopia bubble. I like this.

*

I haven't had a full-length mirror in my home
for most of my adult life. I could even afford
something beautiful and wood framed
these days, but most days it's better
if I don't look at all parts of myself.

INTRODUCTION: STEVEN LEWIS

Unlike my jaw-dropping talented daughter, Elizabeth Bayou-Grace, who revealed to me when she was seven or eight years old that she had the soul of a poet, poetry entered my bloodstream much much later in life. Here's the chronology:

My new freshman roommate at the University of Wisconsin, Dan Depperman, perhaps sensing correctly that I had scuttled my way through high school by copying my girlfriend's homework, informs me that to save my silly shallow suburbanized soul I should write some poetry. I shrug. He's clearly an idiot. Instead, I follow my cool new hipster friends to The Pub on State Street.

Six weeks later, clueless, dateless, depressed, and sloppy drunk, I recall that prescription for my soul and find a napkin, borrow a pencil from the bartender, and begin to scribble a self-absorbed, whiney, pathetic, sing-songy, woe-is-me ode to loneliness.

Minutes later, a slinky girl dressed in black comes over, taps me on my hunched shoulder and asks what I'm doing. I instantly recognize her as one of maybe three or four girls with long black hair, black eyeliner, black turtleneck, black skirt, black tights, and black Pappagallos who refused to dance—or talk—with me an hour before.

So when I tell her somewhat sheepishly that I'm writing a poem, she doesn't turn away without changing expression, as she did when I asked her to dance. She asks what it's about.

I don't tell her it's about my deplorable social life. Or the D's on all my six-week tests. Or my burgeoning understanding that I am not the most special New Yorker that Madison, Wisconsin, has even seen. And while I have not actually read Camus's *The Myth of Sisyphus,* I had apparently awakened momentarily in a 7:45 a.m. freshman comp class to hear someone say something about futility and the meaninglessness of life. >

So I nod to the girl in black and say very somberly, "The meaninglessness of life." And when her head tilts and a sympathetic smile forms on her thin lips, I add, "Futility."

And thereby nab my first college date with Karen Something-or-Other from Detroit.

A few nights later, rather than do the reading for meteorology (a 5-credit class in which I am destined to get a D—and later explain to my outraged parents "You don't need a weatherman to know which way the wind blows"), I return to The Pub, write another bad poem about despair, which I title "Futility II," and another wan creature in black slinks over and wants to know what I'm doing: Date #2.

Accordingly, in the increasingly unkempt and unshorn months to follow, I buy my first army surplus jacket, grow a scraggly goatee, and find that wearing a rolled copy of Siddhartha in my back pocket is a poet's fashion accessory. And yes, I write more terrible poems on more napkins, hoping to attract more black-clad slinky girls who seem to like me for no other reason than I write poems about my utter wretchedness.

*

It was a good gig, playing the miserable poet . . . but as I was soon to find out, it had no staying power. The following fall I arrived back in Madison with my rounded up 2.0 GPA, shaggy as a yak and toting around reams of shamefully shameless poetry in a red rope folder. I stopped by the Pub, set up my writing space in a dark corner . . . and waited. Not one slinky girl in black sidled over. It was 1965. Apparently, misery had been overtaken by anti-war fervor.

Bereft, I scribbled a poorly constructed, self-absorbed, whiney, pathetic woe-is-me sing-songy poem about . . . not being noticed.

I titled it "I Am Invisible I."

No one noticed. And thus began the long—often lonely, more often invisible—odyssey toward discovering the poetry that Dan Depperman might have thought he saw hidden deep beneath my shallow suburbanized soul.

A few years later, arguably far too young to be married or anyone's father, I was not only married and Cael's dad, but lucky enough to get into a poetry class run by the great Ruth Stone at her cottage on Lake Kegonsa . . . where I got schooled on the primacy of the image; and a year or two after that, after we'd stumbled over to Milwaukee, I met the most influential writer I have ever known, the brilliant poet Jim Hazard. Jimmy opened up the front door to his home, his heart and then his poetry tool box to give me a scythe to cut down all the pompous verbiage I had hidden behind as a latter-day Gerard Manley Hopkins. And it was there, on the east side of the dirty Milwaukee River, that I heard the first utterings of a voice to speak the poems that had been hidden, choking in the weeds, my whole life.

Of course that was not the end of my poetry journey. At 75, I can say with some confidence that there is seemingly no end to this dusty path before death overtakes my breath. There were many other, almost always unexpected, lessons to be learned over the next forty years, perhaps none more profound or influential than the week I spent in the Beaufort Memorial Hospital's ICU in March 2020, where utterly ill, isolated and bereft, I barely survived the harrowing effects of Covid-19. Sinking into what I know now as that tremulous wail of existence, the poems in this shared collection with my brilliant daughter were all given voice out of that soul-defining experience. I like to think Dan Depperman would approve.

FROM MY HOSPITAL BED

"... for when I am weak, then I am strong." St. Paul (2 Cor 12:1-10)

So I've wandered this far into the breath-
taking woods, nothing but darkness ahead,
nothing behind except what I think

I remember. Or perhaps made up. I don't
know. Also, I don't know how I know
but I know now there is no path out

of this infinite forest nor why I am
certain there is a fallen tree trunk
up ahead that I will come upon and

sit down, lean over and, pressing my bare
forearms onto my weary thighs, gaze out
through the inscrutable thicket: branches,

leaves, choking vines, waiting for whatever
comes next: animal, rain, morning, hunger,
faith, love, the hunger of love, the everything

and nothing that arrives when prayers
are but childhood wishes, when we know
in our scarred and perfect souls

that what is sacred is profane, profane
sacred, that there is merciful strength
in closing our eyes and welcoming

this illness
of being human
with an unknowing smile.

—SL, Port Royal, SC, May 2020

THROUGH MY HOSPITAL WINDOW

Ten inches. That is my view of the outside world, the ten-inch space between the bottom of the window shade and the sill...

— Neil Selinger, 1953-2011

I. March 2011

My dear friend Neil, being
buried alive in his fading body,
wrote with breathtaking bravery

and grace during his last year of life
through computer-trained retinas
about an ever-diminishing world,

every morning a ten-inch gap
he'd see through the bedroom
window, eyes peering down

past his feet, unable to move
a toe until the nurse would come
to wash and turn and dress him.

II. March 2020

I think of Neil now, trapped
in my own mechanical hospital bed,
IV drips in my arm, oxygen cannula

up my nose, intermittent pneumatic
compression cuffs on my legs, a kind
but unrecognizable nurse in a mask,

gown, and gloves turning me one way
then the other so she can change
the sheets, then giving me unidentified

pills, which I swallow obediently
like a hapless child or a dispirited
rheumy-eyed old man, agreeing

without protest to anything I'm offered:
Jell-O, Mucinex, thermometer, dry chicken,
the daily shot in my stomach.

III. April 2020

While I was on my back in the hospital bed,
time seemed to pass or not pass as in a dream
or a hallucination; and even weeks later

as I lay at home in a weary convalescent
isolation I hardly remember now, I recalled
peering vacantly out the hospital window

when Neil appeared, sat down beside me,
not to offer the usual clichéd consolations,
only to share the narrow view, the private

and solitary darkness illuminated for both
of us by the ten inches he once described
so unforgettably with his eyes alone. Maybe

I imagined it. Perhaps it was a dream.
It's even possible I conjured it up through
this hazy recollection in poetry, but

as we watched cars slowly passing
on Ribaud Road, Spanish moss swaying
languidly from the live oaks, I know I took

one shallow inspiration after another after
another, chest rising, falling, each drawn from
the sweet breath of his long-silenced voice.

—SL, Port Royal, SC, May 2020

THE SAD AND TENDER HEARTS OF WARRIORS (AND BIRDS)

For a brave person, this experience of sad and tender heart is what gives birth to fearlessness.
—Shambhala: The Sacred Path of the Warrior
(Chögyam Trungpa Rinpoche)

I wake this warm spring morning, my window a frame
for the forest of green leaves beyond our yard, mind
fluttering in the breeze of disappearing dreams
whispering Your heart is not hearty, it pulses with fear.

Later, Google tells me a heart is the size of a fist
but I know mine has no knuckles to break a jaw,
thumps like crazy when I'm scared, when I've walked
too quickly up the steps, when I've told a lie.

This tender heart of mine had soared on the thermals
in April when I saw oyster catchers taking turns sitting
on their nest, Sands Beach, Port Royal, three spotted
eggs in a bed of reeds open to all in the hard sand

at the marsh's edge, my fearful spirit swooning
days later after spying a lone egg in the nest, heart
fluttering like a beached fish, one eye staring blindly
into the sun, when I returned to an empty bed

of reeds. I might've fallen to my knees and wailed,
but I did what I've done, turned and pedaled home
hunched over my sad and tender bleeding heart.
A raccoon, we all agreed, doing what raccoons do.

*

>

In early June, my tender heart brimming once more as I
watched a pair of bluebirds set up their wooden house
nailed to a garden post in our backyard in New Paltz, NY,
flying in and out with twigs and grasses, then worms

and insects, until a six-foot black rat snake slithered up
the post, around the baffle I put up to protect against snakes,
bluebird parents squawking and dive bombing to no avail,
the serpent disappearing into the nest to do what snakes do:

eat baby birds. So I awaken this morning to the window
full of leaves, to my heartbroken heart, to whispers of dreams,
wondering what do I do now? Take down the birdhouse?
Leave the woods? Never return to the beach? Kill the snake?

Kill all the snakes in the yard? Trap and drown all raccoons
in Port Royal? I could slink under the covers like a snake
and listen to the rhythm of a weak heart hardened to all
things that snakes and raccoons do, blinding myself against

the sunlit green forest that fills my window each morning,
bluebirds returning to the yard a day after their devastation,
their sad and tender hearts beating furiously, a whisper
on the wind telling them, as me, to do what they do:

eat-sleep-mate, set up a nest, lay eggs, sit on them until
they hatch, feed the chicks until they fledge, or until a storm
blows down the nest; a late spring snow freezes them
solid; a snake or raccoon eats them. And then do it again.

—SL, New Paltz, NY, June 2020

ANOTHER GOOD THING ABOUT ALMOST DYING

For my pal Jeremiah Horrigan, who knows better than I

Bob Marley isn't my name. I don't even know my name yet

—Bob Marley

Alone on the small weathered back deck I just
repainted, gray planks, white rails, glass of red wine
on the black wrought iron table, I'm looking around

through the afternoon slant of sunlight and shadow
at the footprints we've left inside this tree line: swings,
gardens, sheds, playhouse, picnic tables, campfires,

flowerbeds, small pond, the treehouse I can't see around
the bend, recalling the daze of a virus that drove me
to the brink of a dark bottomless lagoon, opening my eyes

to early spring in Port Royal, SC, skinnier, grayer, weaker,
shorter of breath, but the same me, no one else in the bed,
Spanish moss waving languidly outside my window, not

the bare branches of maples and aspens back home.
I did not wake up a new man, reborn or reimagined,
no one other than who I am, the same me returning

to the mountain months later, same husband, father, brother
to the wood turtle I saw this morning, likely headed to a nearby
shale pond, stalled on the road, the two of us with packs on

our backs, ones we've carried around all our lives, mine making
me lean forward, watching my footsteps on the chip and oil
country lane, thumping reminders of my weight on this earth,

my shadow up ahead, echoes of memories left behind, a day

>

older than yesterday, a day closer to the edge of the pond
as I would have been, virus or no virus, and like the turtle,

I am in no rush to get there, pack sliding off my back as I sit on
an ice age boulder to rest, to consider and reconsider the house,
gardens, sheds, swings, treehouse, the timpani of crickets and birds

that will someday follow the turtle slipping soundlessly into
the dark water, swimming down to the warm mucky bottom
where we are, each of us, nameless, eternally ourselves.

— SL, New Paltz, June 2020

TIME TO STEP INTO THE LIGHT AGAIN

I foresaw that in the blinding sunshine of that land I would become acquainted with a flabby, pretending, weak-eyed devil of a rapacious and pitiless folly.

—Joseph Conrad, *Heart of Darkness*

Time to step into the light again.

Time to leave this warm yellow house ringed with porches
like a moat. Time to bike out of the deep green woods,

to wander up Main Street as before, to grab a burger at P&Gs,
find a shady, lonely spot on the rail trail, lower the bandanna,
and then, finally, finally time to bite into juicy life once more,

to wipe my chin with the back of my hand, then wipe my hand
on my shorts like the ageless boy who still lives in my dark past
and meanders down by the river, squinting from the sharp
sunlight, but led along now by an illuminating darkness I have

learned to trust as a guide, here a simple reminder of the faith
I'll need to return to our shared daytime nightmares, the shameless
lies uttered in broad daylight by the devils in boardrooms and pulpits
and courtrooms and newsrooms and Senate chambers and rose
gardens everywhere. This is no time to turn away from the false

prophets behind emoji faces who sneer at the anguish all around.
No time to salute the false prophets of patriotism who treat warriors
as fodder in some despicable battle for hideous profit and power.
No time to invest in profiteers making billions off wars, drugs,
prisons, poverty, the pathetic lies that feed a flabby pandemic

of hatred, cowardice, and fear. No time like now to walk again
with the huddled masses yearning to breathe free, the wretched
refuse, the unwelcome immigrants we've now become in our own
land, prisoners interrogated under the glare of self-righteousness,

>

each of us a slave to the liars, con artists, traitors, thieves robbing
us of life, liberty, and the wholesome pursuit of happiness
with fake promises, phony flickering neon slogans

blinding us from the Golden Rule, the only truth
that will save us from ourselves.

–SL, New Paltz, NY, July 2020

WEDNESDAY ON THE PORCH

Back on the front porch
after biking into town,
walking the river to ridge
trail with an old friend,
biking home, t-shirt

soaked with sweat, cold
well water splashed
on my face, stinging eyes
closed on the weary glory
of an ordinary summer day

only to feel a tick burrowing
into my leg, then one on my
arm, then another and another,
five tiny bloodsuckers feasting
on my flesh, five pulse-quickening

reminders that even in this easy
July oasis, momentarily separated
from the uneasy cares of the never
easy world by a fortress of trees,
safety is an illusion, that I wake

each day no different than any
creature that walks on earth, flies
through air, swims in water
without a prayer, every breath
a miracle that comes upon me

unearned, tick by tock, tick by
tick, not by the grace of anyone's
narrow scripture, but through some
holy knowledge, alive in the wind,
breathing in, breathing out,

even as I flush the menacing
uncrushable ticks down the toilet
and call the doc for doxycycline,
I must thank each doomed wriggling
bug for its unintended reminder

to be watchful, to be humble,
to remember that safety is death,
that life arrives in a gasp, tick by tick
burrowing under the skin, that grace
never comes to anyone for the asking.

—SL, New Paltz, NY, July 2020

AROUND THE BEND

For Clay, Devin, Bella, Connor, Rory, Maddie, Schuyler, Jack,
Charlee, Eleanor, Cade, Bridger, Emma, Hattie, Maggie, Delilah

I've clipped the low branches on the magnolia we planted in '85,
so you can now sit on the front porch, see past the mossy lawn
into the woods and halfway down the long shale driveway before
it curves away toward our dog and cat cemetery, right where
Sammy the cat would leap out of the bush and scare kids
walking to the long-gone bus shelter on Cragswood Road.

*

I was sitting in a green porch rocker yesterday, savoring the new view,
phoebes swooping in and out of nests in the eaves, remembering how
our oldest grandkid, Clay, once said, "I used to think it was Craps-woods,
but now I know it's Woods-craps," which still makes me smile and I say it
out loud so I can hear the little boy voice again uttering his new truth.

And so it goes, years later, that this quiet country lane is occasionally called
Craps-woods around the tribe, those who were among us when he said it,
and those who appeared like skinny spotted fawns wandering out from the
forest to later hear the tale of how a word gets convoluted, becomes part
of the landscape until the view curves and whatever was there lingers

as it goes around the bend. Like now, more than halfway into this wholly
unholy miserable year of illness, death, lies, and despair turning into the
regretful past, so many of us still isolated behind walls, masks, gloves,
fogging eyeglasses, breathless in blind fear of what is coming next, it is
heartening to sit on this porch, to see a little further down the shady drive,

mind wandering into woods, into wonder, past the lies, the twisted words
and images corrupting our eternal truths, yet how ironic that it's 2020
and, low branches cleared, I am again seeing 20-20, far enough ahead
to imagine my grandchildren on the cliff at Bonticou Crag, sixteen kids
with their arms around each other's shoulders, singing Johnny Nash's

"I Can See Clearly Now," luminous eyes opened to the sorrowful truth that the elders of this great nation have failed them, have allowed wrong to be right, unholy to be holy, sweet voices traveling on thermals down toward Woods-craps Road, past the cemetery, around the curve to me rocking and singing along with shame, pride, and hope that they will turn truth back on itself before I disappear around the bend.

—SL, New Paltz, NY, July 2020

FOR EVER

One generation passeth away, and *another* generation cometh:
—Ecclesiastes 1:4

Returning from the Low Country in May, from COVID-19, twelve-
foot gators in the pond, home to the Shawangunk Mountains, yard
overgrown, overrun with chipmunks, chipmunks digging holes
in gardens, in the driveway, chipmunks undermining the foundation,
chipmunks running fearlessly over our feet on the back deck.

In June I recoiled from a black rat snake disappearing into the barn,
then a pair mating near the garden, one slithering out of a hole
in the base of a pine, seven feet long, thick as an underground cable,
then another falling out of the barn loft with a thud at Patti's feet in July,
another curled on the screen porch, still another at the front door.

It is August now, dawn, and I'm looking out the bedroom window, one
solitary chipmunk scurrying near the swingset, maybe a sign this plague
of snakes has done its ancient job, and when I turn to see if Patti is still
asleep, the curve of her hip under the blanket as stirring as it has been
through the countless quiet intimacies no one knows but us, the dizzying

chaos of life with seven kids, the unquiet quiet after they'd moved on,
moving ever onward to this early morning as I scan the yard for danger,
an unfamiliar smile cracking my watchful face as I realize that my
biblical terror of serpents has moved along with the chipmunks, that
this generation of vipers, despite so few predators in these woods,

will eventually move along, if not today then around the bend, when
cold November forces them into dark dens until next Spring when they
will find more plentiful yards and gardens, leaving Patti and me alone
together again, whatever unforeseen perils or joys come our way,
wherever we plant our feet on the earth, whenever we move along.

SL, New Paltz, NY, August 2020

FIFTY-TWO YEARS

41 summers on this beach, weeks now without the kids,
all of them hunkering down closer to home, behind masks,
elbow to elbow hellos, quiet lakes, swimming pools,
creeks, a soundless sound, little but time for us now
to walk barefoot along this shifting barrier island, time
to gaze at the never silent sea, willets' piercing calls, ruddy
turnstones skittering back from each crashing wave, brown
pelicans dive bombing into the swells, the swells roaring
to shore, ghost crabs disappearing in holes in the sand.

52 years ago we were younger than our oldest grandson,
barely out of our teens, vowing for all to hear an eternal love
we could not possibly understand, would not realize until
words proved useless to explain how more than five decades
would pass and we'd still be here, still Patti & Steve, Steve &
Patti, still a mystery to each other, mystifying how far we've
wandered down this sandy strand, encircled by the arc
of an inscrutable ocean, and with no sage advice to offer
young lovers, we now sit quietly, side by side in rusting beach

chairs, this unfathomable life no less a mystery than the relentless
sea or why our rinky dink cottage behind the hurricane-flattened
dunes, named for a surfing dog long dead, is still standing
on its 8-foot pilings, still rocking through dozens of vicious storms,
endless nor'easters taking cottage after cottage into the surf,
a mystery how she's welcomed us home for 41 summers, a howling
wind of joy through countless nights of shrimp, blue crabs, oysters,
clams, spoon bread, hush puppies, beer, wine, the photos of 7 kids,
7 spouses, 16 grandkids on the light green wall behind our table.

SL, Hatteras Island, NC, August 2020

FROM A RUSTED BEACH CHAIR

Walk on air against your better judgment.
—Seamus Heaney, 1939-2013

My dear friend JJ sends an email to me, alone
on this barrier island beach, with a quote
about a writer's struggle, "a snarled confusion
of suffering, without redemption." In other words,
he, who is a superb writer, despairs his work
is going nowhere, is lost at sea. Me

mesmerized by the crashing waves, eight months
into a year of misery purged on the page, I suspect
that redemption for any of us, writers, criminals,
politicians, anyone who makes of language a boat
untethered from the dock, tangled rope flopping
in the choppy sea, the days and nights, sun and wind,

swells and rain, coming as offerings we don't choose,
just to welcome into our embrace. Or not. Here
at the edge of the warm green Atlantic, no scrotum
tightening sea this, watching children in the rollers,
surfers riding swells into shore, falling backward into
the children's foam. Not a bad place to spend a pandemic,

to see between blinks of an eye, the vast space in the seam,
the pretty girl out beyond the breakers, sitting straight up
straddling her board, who doesn't find the wave, the wave
coming to her, and when she stands, long arms outstretched,
she leans in, gives herself over to the current without thought,
without fear, gliding on air toward the crashing shore.

SL, Hatteras Island, NC, August 2020

STANDING IN THE EYE

You can dance in a hurricane
But only if you're standing in the eye
—Brandi Carlile

Looks like it's raining up near Oregon Inlet,
dark clouds north from this stretch of beach
in Rodanthe where the sun is shining over
clear azure water and they're hauling in
mackerel, mullet, and cobia on the pier.
For this moment, all is well in the world,

despite all that is wrong in the world, things
far more disheartening than the massive piles
of sand along Ocean Drive from the April
nor'easter or the condemned cottage that once
stood fifty yards from the dune before Hurricane
Isabel in 2003, these days teetering in the surf

at high tide. Someone's small tragedy. But for now
I'm sitting in the sun, feet in the sand, watching
the hazy screen of rain up north, singing to myself
"You don't need a weatherman to know which way
the wind blows," and trying to recall long gone days
before the 2003 storm, the peaceful empty beach,

sea oats waving in the dunes even while all hell was
breaking loose in Iraq after the hellish lies were told,
our boys and girls wearing flak jackets in the sand,
the beginning of the end of our national faith
in naked truth, the squalid shows of false patriotism
to follow, the shameless indecency of our leaders,

and yet there was also redemption at home that May,
Clover and Jeffrey getting married by the stream
in New Paltz, how we laughed and danced in the eye

>

of a hurricane we didn't see coming in September, how
it washed away the WPA dunes, four feet of sand under
the cottage to be dug out by hand, our youngest kids

in crisis, American boys and girls overseas besieged
by mortars, missiles, IEDs, car bombs, RPGs, and worse,
the cruel lies of cynical politicians counting their
thirty pieces of silver, five hundred dead by Christmas,
the foul-smelling winds of an endless war still
circling this enduring barrier island, this sanctuary

from which there is no lasting sanctuary, just a
sunny respite from storms gathering north and south,
east and west, the graveyard of the Atlantic, its
five thousand ships buried in the shoals, the souls
of unsung sailors singing through the gusting wind
reminding us there is time, always time, to lean back

in a rusted beach chair under blue skies, the arc
of heaven and ocean out ahead, waves ever crashing
after crashing, time to recall how love blossomed
in the gazebo by the stream, how we danced into
darkness, why I must now dive into the sparkling sea
like a child, tiny silver fish darting through the swells.

SL, Hatteras Island, NC, August 2020

RIMA ASKS WHY THREE LINE STANZAS

Something lifts our wings ....
–Rumi

When speaking of birth and death
and the everything in between,
the doleful beginnings, the middle,

the ends of these harrowing days,
there are only three elements:
the female, the male, the holy other,

each one beholden to, flowing
through, the other two, what
the early mystics must have known

in their hearts but misunderstood
its eternal embrace, leaving out
women in their narrow, selfish

view of the immemorial triptych
of the planet: earth, water, the wind
that dear-dear-dear Emily whispered

through her own trinity: *First – Chill –*
then Stupor – then the letting go –
and so here I find myself in this poem,

still seeking blessed air, each breath
a gift for the aching lungs, the tender
heart, oxygen for rivers of blood

flowing through these arteries,
each exhale a grateful surrender
to the everything, the sum, the all

I misunderstood, I seem to almost
understand now, yet still
have no earthly idea why

>

I did not drown in the roiling
waters. Maybe it just doesn't matter.
As my dear friend Larry told me,

"Where you stepped in the river
is not across from where
you are crawling up the bank."

SL, Hatteras Island, NC, August 2020

ODE TO THIS FRAIL BODY

For Leigh and Isabel who wondered

So you find yourself
lying in a hospital bed
on your back, needles
in your arm, cannula
up your nose, intermittent
pneumatic compression
devices on your legs,
and you're staring up
into the darkness, when
some 3 a.m. voice arrives
like a drunk call, or maybe
like some nightshift orderly,
a former professional athlete
in gown and gloves who
empties the waste basket
and says behind a mask,

If you make it through
the night, there will be
no standing ovation
awaiting you in the morning.
There are no fourth quarter
Hail Marys that make any
difference in this life, silly man,
no prizes, no film contracts,
no eureka, no aha, nothing
ahead but the flesh and some
daily practice, something you
do every day as sustenance,
as a reminder among other
daily reminders like hunger,
that you do not exist at the behest
of who you think you are passing
through this life, you are here
at the merciful mercy of the frail

>

and tender body in which you live,
in which you have always lived,
as you were in the beginning
and as you will be at the end.

And in that moment of darkness,
you see that no matter what
you've done between your first
yowling breath and this dark night,
there has been no sanctum outside
the body, that even if you rise
from the bed, shed the hospital gown,
and dance wildly in the moonlight
to the pulsing light on the monitor,
passing ghosts in the hallway,
and enter the world beyond
which only blasphemers dare
describe, there is still only this
sickly body to render you alive.

So you take a shallow breath and wait
patiently for morning, where your daily
practice awaits you, some sweet devotion
without purpose beyond itself, beyond
superstition, even beyond hope, leading
you closer and closer to some fleeting
reconciliation for the day you are alive,
some breath of labor or art or prayer
that begins to fade the instant you breathe
into it, even as it burrows by rote under
your skin, pulses through your arteries,
the in and out of your aching lungs.

—SL, Hatteras Island, NC, August 2020

WE WALK ON THE BEACH AFTER GETTING A LETTER FROM HATTIE

Driving rain all morning, windswept beach, weather.com
says tropical systems coming out of West Africa, Cape Verde,
waves leaping over the sand shelf that appeared last night,
and this afternoon as I skitter back from the roiling surf
like a sanderling, I am already shaking my head at the way
events begun thousands of miles away might splash the hem
of my shorts days later; then glancing toward my wife Patti
I marvel how love begins and survives across five decades,
luminous days and nights, countless storms, some born long
long before love began, others eons before our first breaths . . .

And all that before returning to the cottage, before facing this
computer, still thinking about Cape Verde, then wondering
where poems come from, why they keep coming, even as
I'm partway into this one without a clue to where it's headed
or what I hope, if hope is the right word, comes after it's written,
a willet flying off with that piercing call, bold black and white
markings on the underside of its wings, which is when I notice
the envelope on the desk from ten year old Hattie (Hatteras Patricia)
who wrote a letter (Damma & Chiefie, PO Box 14), telling us
that she hates ". . . this mind boggling pandemic,"

the "unknowingness" of it all. So I leave the poem behind
to cross oceans of blood and love, to write back, to reach up
the coast, to say "Damma and I totally get it." And when she texts,
"Thanks! Glad u get it" . . . adding the sweat emoji, I think Whew!
For Hattie. For both of us. For all of us. For all the unanswerable truths
of love and storms spawned in mystery, currents above and below
the waves, swells crossing the Gulf Stream, wild winds passing over
this barrier island, its endless unknowingness felt from my bare feet
in wet sand, leaping up over my knees, as I skitter back to the mind
boggling poetry, the words our dear Hatteras speaks for the ages.

—SL, Hatteras Island, NC/New Paltz, NY, Sept. 2020

ATONEMENT ON FLOWER MOUNTAIN

Suddenly—and that's no literary suddenly—
I wonder who or what this cemetery is named for.
So I take the easy Wiki route, find Montefiore:
". . . Sephardi Jews . . . from the Iberian Peninsula
. . . Meaning *"flower mountain,"* which is where
my old pal Jonnie is buried (Block 5, Section 2),

and deeper into this city of the dead, around
the circle, then down Montefiore Avenue
are my parents, all my aunts and uncles,
a few cousins (Block 12, Section 6). Once

a year I drive down to Flower Mountain
. . . to remember? not forget? do my duty?
pay my respects? Maybe just to put my arms
around the shoulders of my living old friends,
Richard and Jim, as we laugh over misspent
youth, smile over the foibles of our missing

buddy, our lost third baseman, until it's time
to drive off, up the narrow road, around
the circle, where there is no laughter left in me,
not along the gravel path passing headstones

engraved with names I know from before I knew
my pals, no smile even when I reach my parents'
graves, Samuel I. and Lillian A., Beloved Father-
Mother, Grandfather-Grandmother, Great Grandfather-
Great Grandmother, no grin as I lay pebbles
on the markers and stand before them, still the same

stone-faced boy they would remember, a cry caught
in my throat turning into a hoarse whisper, an unwritten
novel, unspoken words edited down to "I'm sorry" and
moments later, just my lips moving now, ". . . I'm sorry."

—SL, New Paltz, NY, September 2020

LIKE THEIR MOTHERS

So much chatter on these unseasonably warm
November days about redemption, as if God
or god or the gods or whatever mysterious
forces in the cosmos would ever ever choose
a politician, any politician, as a redeemer.

Yes, I'm breathing better, but there is nothing
otherworldly different than last week, except
the weather; the car still needs bearings, house
could still use a power wash and a coat of paint,
I still love my wife and kids with all my heart,

just as I will next week when the last leaves
drift from their bare trees, when rain water will
again trickle out of downspouts, Thanksgiving,
Christmas, snows, another year, another spring,
summer, fall, right on schedule, just like last year,

and though that is not redemption in a country
as riven as this one, rifts deep as the magnificent
Grand Canyon, as long and occasionally
unpassable as the Continental Divide, today
is still a good day—and nothing is more heartening,

more satisfying, than to be alive and sitting here
on the porch surrounded by sleeping woods
as all my girls—Bella, Maddie, Charlee, Eleanor,
Emma, Hattie, Maggie, Delilah—are seeing a new
vice president who looks like their mothers.

—SL, New Paltz, NY, November 2020

STILL WE GATHER TOGETHER

"Can we perceive those inorganic beings, don Juan?" I asked.
"We certainly can," he replied. "Sorcerers do it at will. Average people do it, but they don't realize that they're doing it because they are not."
—Carlos Castenada

Through this flash flooding autumn pandemic
full of more worries than a deadly virus,
it's that deadly virus alone that has propelled
Patti and me rafting downstream to Hatteras
for Thanksgiving, leaving behind beloved
children and grandchildren jumping up
and waving as we pass, stranded on
their own safe and lonesome shores. Now

on this windswept island, rafts of muscle memory
keep blowing me back home: I'm down in Avon
picking up groceries and suddenly swinging baby
Cael (now 51) up on my hip; clutching a bag
of bird seed and rocking Nancy (47) in my arms
as she turns her tiny face into my chest; grinning
at a sweet baby girl crying in a grocery cart,
and there's Addie (almost 45), head out, body
unborn, wailing her imminent arrival, everyone
in the delivery room laughing with me;

and so it goes, walking the beach, shoveling sand,
grabbing a beer from the fridge, reaching through
the driver's side window, Clover (43) sliding into
my bare hands upstairs on Coffey Lane, her first
breath; Danny (41) birthed between my legs
as Patti sits on my lap at the edge of the bed;
fingers cupping Bay's (35) little ear, warm cheek
in the hollow beneath my shoulder and we dance
around the new house; my arm around Patti nursing
baby Elizabeth (32), Nancy, Addie, Clover, Danny
crowding the room at the hospital on 2nd Avenue.

Even now as I stand alone at the edge of the quiet
surf, the heavy flapping song of a brown pelican
lifting off, soaring over the swells, a laryngeal spasm
has me singing off-key into the lonely wind, "We
gather together to ask the Lord's blessing . . . ," lyrics
on gravy-stained paper, handed out each year around
the long crowded table, always followed by groans,
real and forced, always a joke and never a joke,
deadly virus or not, nowhere and everywhere
on this beach, cochlear reverberations of sweet
voices in my inner ear, the muscular ocean,
here and there, forever rushing to shore.

–SL, Hatteras Island, November 2020

AMAZING GRACE

For weeks I've been listening to Aaron Neville's
Amazing Grace, in the car, on the porch, riding
my bike, over and over like some lovesick teen,
the voice of snow melt sluicing down the mountain,
rippling past the gazebo, the tree house, small
sparkling rapids as unexpected tears spill down

my craggy cheeks this morning, over my unshaven
jaw, pooling in my chest where I relive, time and
again, the sweet sadness of rocking babies to sleep,
inhaling the nectarous soft spot on their tiny skulls—
never enough, never enough, ever—ever knowing
how fleeting is bliss, that grace, like mountain water,

cannot be contained in the palms of our hands, even
as it pauses in puddles and ponds moving ever on to
the ocean of sky, even as some try to claim it as their
own, as if grace could be deeded, bartered, dammed
against some imaginary drought, this brief flowing
purl of Aaron Neville calling us all to devotions.

—SL, New Paltz, NY, November 2020

ODE TO NOTHING: A NOVEMBER RUMINATION

"Nothing from nothing leaves nothing"
croons Billy Preston, and I'm happy enough
to sing along on this early morning and agree
with the emotional arithmetic of that line,

even though I wonder if it adds up when I turn
off the ignition, glancing around at leafless trees,
dead vines, stalks in the garden, juncos flying
into feeders, still calculating as I get out, leaving

footprints in the rain-soaked grass, reminders
of writing work to be done before lunch, leaves
raked in the afternoon, after the sun comes out,
before the sun sets behind the ridge, bills to be

paid, the quiet night ahead, just us, alone again,
on the couch, feet up on the coffee table, the only
time in the long and short day when nothing
is transactional, when the stupid tv program

on the screen is just a stupid tv program, and later
when the book I'm reading in bed, sheets cold
then warm, is just a book, not a primer, when
nothing from nothing is never nothing.

—SL, New Paltz, NY, November 2020

ART ON THE OTHER SIDE: A SONNET

"The hope is that if you live through it, there will be art on the other side,"
—Louise Glück

When we learn there is no art on this side of the river,
just smooth talkin' tv jive about miracle drugs, sweet
voiceovers listing deadly side effects, then we see
that all we have ever done is dip our toes in the holy

creek, stepping back reflexively, quaking in some
faithless belief that salvation is to be found in con
artists who profit from our desperation, promising
miracles, but only for those afraid of drowning,

supplicants huddled on the naked shore, chained in
hopeless hatred for the undaunted who have waded
in. Only then. Only then do we step into the rushing
current and, floating downstream, grab hold of a root,

a branch, another's hand, and crawl up on the other shore,
where art is alive between the canopy and the forest floor

SL, New Paltz, NY, November 2020

THREE DAYS AFTER THANKSGIVING

"The way of love is not
a subtle argument.
The door there
is devastation.
—Rumi

I'm leaning on the rail of the Rodanthe pier,
willing a loggerhead to paddle by, although
I'd be happy enough to see a puppy drum reeled
in by the guys casting on either side of me.

But it's the loggerhead I really want, so I press
my forearms into the rough rail, gouged along
the edges for rods, soaked through with seasons
of cut squid, shrimp, mullet, blood worms,

and wait, swells passing below, shaking the pier
the way someone around me might be shuddering
in fear, in sickness, in lost love, then close my eyes
as if there's some unspoken incantation to be found

in the dark, invoking the turtle to be there when
I re-open my eyelids into this picture perfect
afternoon, Carolina blue skies, warm sun, blue
ocean, but still no turtle, which is when I see a flash

below and follow a line cast out on a rod leaning
on the rail, a live bait hooked through its tail, wriggling
in desperate circles, and in that mesmerizing moment,
I know what the tethered fish doesn't know: the pain

of the hook ripping from its tailfin is the price for
the dance of gratitude I will see in its shimmering
scales moments before it disappears below the rolling
swells that make this pier shudder again . . . and again.

—SL, Hatteras Island, NC, Nov./Dec. 2020

FOUR DAYS AFTER THANKSGIVING

Birds make great sky-circles
of their freedom.
How do they learn it?
They fall, and falling,
they're given wings."
— Mawlana Jalal-al-Din Rumi

I'm standing barefoot in cool sand.
Behind me devastation from
Hurricane Isaias, the nor'easters
that wouldn't go away, waves
lapping at pilings of cottages
destined to collapse into the sea.

In front of me, inscrutable ocean,
hundreds—maybe thousands—
of cormorants flying in a jagged
unbroken broken line from south
to north, soaring over swells past
the end of the pier, where yesterday

I waited in vain to see a loggerhead,
where I had to remind myself again
(again!) that there is godhood
in this tragically sunny mess
of a universe, in the condemned
cottages behind me, in the exhilarating

flight of cormorants, a fin gliding
between the swells, a cloud the shape
of a pelican, something true beyond
all true reckoning, something
that creates everything, destroys
everything, every day an unbroken

broken line, a riptide in a child's
ocean of joy that takes more than it
gives, gives more than any of us can
bear, a force that does not, will not,
save us from ourselves, but washes
my feet with every crashing wave.

—SL, Hatteras Island, NC,
Nov./Dec. 2020

A WEEK AFTER THANKSGIVING

Something opens our wings. Something makes boredom and hurt disappear.
Someone fills the cup in front of us: We taste only sacredness.
— Mawlana Jalal-al-Din Rumi

After my writing practice on this dreary December morning,
there is little to do after lunch, no more mowing, leaves blown
past the tree line, fences put up against hungry deer in January,
repairs on the barn put off until mud season, just the vast tundra
of winter ahead, boots left at the door, scarves stuffed in arms

of jackets hung on hooks, ceiling lights warding off early afternoon
shadows, oil burner rumbling as I stand in the archway, glance
around this still life of a living room, empty couch, unlit fireplace,
blank tv screen, six uninhabited bedrooms on the second and third
floors above my head, and when I turn around to peer across

the dim hall into the quiet kitchen, cold coffee in the pot, breakfast
crumbs on the counter, dishes in the white porcelain sink, refrigerator
humming . . . I take a deep breath and wonder if I have courage enough
to brave the cold afternoons ahead without boredom or despair or empty
calories. Am I brave enough to marvel at the slant of light through frosty

windows onto the yellowed lawn, bare brown trees? Am I audacious
enough to find pointless solace in the crunch of gravel as I amble out
to the mailbox and, zipping up against the wind, keep walking along
the quiet road to one trail or another, only to return to this yellow
house in the woods before dark, red cheeked, eyes glistening,

and light a fire, pour some cabernet, sit in the silent living room
before dinner with Patti and talk . . . or not talk. Do I have the grit,
the daring, the spunk to savor the coming dark and chilly afternoons
without wishing away this hibernating paradise that asks nothing
of me except that I welcome it into my sacred heart each day?

–SL, New Paltz, NY, December 2020

SITTING UNDER A LIVE OAK IN PORT ROYAL, SC CONSIDERING THE BLANK PAGE

Kind of odd to be pondering the blank page
at this late date, right? I mean, it's long past
the time to start being interested in empty
spaces when I've lived my life in the midst

of dizzying abundance, when I can see age
spots polka-dotting my hands while I type
this poem, when practically every page in the
notebook of my life is scribbled with indelible

ink. I mean, why start now when I've never before
found an empty page daunting. Nor have I ever
thought about entering into white space as a battle,
like my warrior poet daughter Elizabeth, though

I know in my bones the ugliness and chaos she
must face in the face of empty spaces, even now
on this formerly blank page—which, by the way,
is of course still lurking behind these words—

here I am mulling blank spaces as if they are
undiscovered rooms in dreams, placeless places
to sit without expectation, without demand,
perhaps the only spaces in what is now a long life

where I might walk past the security guards
at the door and, without map or guide or gun,
give myself over to the void, enter into a virgin
forest without destination, without knowledge

of what I might come upon, or come upon me,
some place to sit on a downed log
and say "Oh." Not "Aha." Just
"Oh."

—SL, Port Royal, SC, April 2021

ACKNOWLEDGMENTS

First and foremost, a big thank you to my first poetry teacher, my father, for co-writing this collection with me. It's really an honor to share this work with you. And a thanks to the many teachers who came after him, especially: Kevin Cothren, Gary Hawkins, Catherine Reid, Erin Stalcup, Kathleen Peirce, Steve Wilson, and Kate Senecal. Thank you for nurturing my poet heart and for giving me the courage to find my own voice. Also, a thank you to the Pioneer Valley Writer's Workshop for providing so many of us with a community of writers and the space to get work done, especially during these trying, isolated times. Finally, I would love to thank my family. To my mother, for endless support, acceptance, and love. To my siblings, for giving me a whole cast of people to look up to. And to my husband, Ryan, for being the absolute best partner to survive a pandemic with. Thank you for the laughter, the patience, the encouragement, the music, and of course, the many, many delicious meals. I love you.

–EBG, Easthampton, MA

Grateful acknowledgment is due to this extraordinary family of ours, 32 strong, who support us, encourage us, indulge us, warn us, welcome us, laugh with us, laugh at us, comfort us, and urge us to be as courageous as they are, to write the truth.

–SL, New Paltz, NY

"The First Winter," "Remembering the Day Before My Marriage," and "Fire in Paradise" were first published in *Sixfold Poetry* (Winter 2020 issue).

"Another Good Thing About Almost Dying" was first published in *Intima* (Fall 2020). In addition, several poems in this collection were first published as podcasts at Read650.org.